ONCE UPON A FAIRY TALE
The Stolen Slipper
STORY BY
Anna Staniszewski
ART BY
Macky Pamintuan
BRANCHES™
SCHOLASTIC INC.

Once Upon a Fairy Tale

Help Kara and Zed fix all the fairy tales!
Once Upon a Fairy Tale
The Magic Mirror
Anna Staniszewski
Macky Pamintuan
Scholastic
Once Upon a Fairy Tale
The Stolen Slipper
Anna Staniszewski
Macky Pamintuan
Scholastic
Once Upon a Fairy Tale
The Missing Dwarf
Anna Staniszewski
Macky Pamintuan
Scholastic
Once Upon a Fairy Tale
The Snoring Princess
Anna Staniszewski
Macky Pamintuan
Scholastic

TABLE OF CONTENTS

For Lia – AS

For Ali, my brave princess – MP

Library of Congress Cataloging-in-Publication Data

Names: Staniszewski, Anna, author.
Title: The stolen slipper / Anna Staniszewski.
Description: First edition. | New York : Branches/Scholastic Inc., 2019. | Series: Once upon a fairy tale ; 2 | Audience: Ages 6-8. | Audience: Grades 2-3. | Summary: Frustrated in his search for the lady who belongs to the glass slipper, Prince Patrick turns to Kara's father, the shoemaker, to ask who made the glass slippers; it can only have been a fairy godmother, but Kara is determined to help, and she enlists her friend Zed and his pet goat in the search— an adventure that could end up with the children thrown into the dungeon, because there is a conspiracy afoot, and the chief conspirator is in the heart of the palace. Identifiers: LCCN 2019027553 (print) | LCCN 2019027554 (ebook) | ISBN 9781338349757 (paperback) | ISBN 9781338349764 (hardcover) | ISBN 9781338349771 (ebook)
Subjects: LCSH: Cinderella (Tale)—Juvenile fiction. | Glass shoes—Juvenile fiction. | Theft—Juvenile fiction. | Conspiracies—Juvenile fiction. | Adventure stories. | Fantasy. | CYAC: Characters in literature—Fiction. | Shoes—Fiction. | Stealing—Fiction. | Conspiracies—Fiction. | Adventure and adventurers—Fiction. | LCGFT: Fantasy fiction. | Action and adventure fiction.
Classification: LCC PZ7.S78685 Mi 2020 (print) | LCC PZ7.S78685 (ebook) | DDC 813.6 [Fic]—dc23
LC record available at https://lccn.loc.gov/2019027553
LC ebook record available at https://lccn.loc.gov/2019027554

10 9 8 7 6 5 4 3 2 1 19 20 21 22 23

Printed in China 62
First edition, December 2019
Illustrated by Macky Pamintuan
Edited by Erin Black
Book design by Sarah Dvojack

1
Searching for a Shoe

"Kara! Are you reading back here again?" her father asked. He peeked his head into the storeroom of their family shoe shop.

Kara popped out from behind a shelf. "I found a book about the Dragon Lands," she said. "I can't wait to visit there someday."

Her father laughed. "You have plenty to see right here in the Enchanted Kingdom—like boys who bring pet goats inside shoe shops."

Kara's face lit up. "Zed!" She hurried to the front of the store.

Her best friend, Zed, was at the counter, eating cookies meant for customers. He was lucky Kara's mother was too busy measuring an ogre's foot to notice.

"Do you need directions again?" Kara asked.

"Yep," he said. "One day, I'll stop getting lost." He took a scroll of paper from his messenger bag and held it out to her.

Zed was a royal messenger, which meant he delivered letters for princes and queens. Kara thought his job sounded a lot more exciting than selling shoes.

"Leprechaun Lane is easy to find!" Kara said, reading the address. "It's past Gingerbread House Way, just before the Wishing Pond."

Kara loved studying maps almost as much as she loved reading about faraway lands. She drew a quick map for Zed. When she was done, Zed's goat, Nina, tried to nibble the pen.

"Shoo!" Zed said, batting her away.

"Couldn't you leave Nina at home?" Kara asked.

"I tried," Zed said. "She's as stubborn as you are."

"Kara," her mother said. "The shop floor isn't going to sweep itself!"

"It would if you bought a magic broom," Kara said. She grabbed a non-magical broom and started sweeping by Zed's feet. Then she asked him, "Don't you need to hurry and deliver your letter?"

"Nah," Zed said, biting into another cookie. "It's just another message about Prince Patrick's search for his true love."

Everyone knew the story of the mystery lady from the royal ball. She had danced with the prince all night, and he had fallen in love with her. But at midnight, she had run out of the castle, leaving behind a glass slipper.

"I hope they find her," Zed went on. "I'm tired of delivering these messages!"

"At least you're part of an adventure," Kara said. She liked helping out at the shoe shop, but she wanted to explore and save the day!

"Who needs adventure? I wouldn't want to miss Gram's vegetable potpie tonight," Zed said. "Plus, I have to find a home for my baby hedgehog. Gram says if I bring in another stray, she'll make me sleep in the barn."

Kara smiled. Zed had two hobbies: eating and befriending stray animals.

The bell above the door jingled. A young man strode in. He was tall and had a sword hanging at his hip.

"Stay," the man told a brown puppy at his heel. The dog sat outside the shop. Behind him, a gleaming horse and carriage waited.

"Your Highness!" Kara's mother cried. She dipped into a curtsy. Kara's father bowed.

Kara's mouth fell open. Prince Patrick himself was standing in her parents' shop!

2
A Glass Slipper

"How may we help you, sire?" Kara's mother asked.

"I'm looking for a shoe," Prince Patrick said.

"Of course," Kara's father said. "We'll start by measuring your feet."

"No, I don't need to *buy* shoes," the prince explained. "I need to find a shoe that was stolen from my library last week. It's a glass slipper."

Kara and Zed exchanged a look. No wonder the search for the mystery lady was taking so long. If there was no shoe to match, the prince would never be able to find who had the other glass slipper!

"How can we help?" Kara's father asked.

"This is what the shoe looks like," the prince said, holding up a drawing. "Do you know who could have made it?"

Kara's father scratched his beard in thought. "It must have been a fairy godmother."

"Only magic can turn glass into shoes," Kara's mother said.

The prince pulled off his hat and twisted it like a wet rag. "Dozens of fairies live in this kingdom. How will I find the right one?"

At that moment, Nina snatched the hat out of the prince's hand. "Nina, no!" Zed cried. But the goat swallowed the hat in one gulp.

Prince Patrick only laughed and said to Zed, "My dog, Duncan, is a nibbler, just like your goat." He pointed outside to where the puppy was chewing on a stick. The prince turned back to Kara's parents. "Thank you for your help."

Kara's stomach squeezed as she watched Prince Patrick walk out the door. Adventure didn't come into Kara's life every day. She couldn't let it leave!

She ran after the prince. "Sire! Please wait!" she cried.

"Yes, what is it?" he asked.

"I'll help you!" Kara said. "I'll find the stolen slipper."

Too Many Cooks?

"*You* will find the slipper?" Prince Patrick asked. "Aren't you a little young to solve crimes?"

"I grew up around shoes," Kara said proudly. "I'm the perfect person for the job!"

"I'll ask my chief adviser," the prince said. He turned toward the carriage. Inside, a small man with a large necktie was hunched over a scroll. "Barth?"

The man was so busy writing his letter, he didn't seem to hear Prince Patrick.

"Barth!" the prince said, knocking on the carriage door.

The man jumped. "My apologies," he said. "I was writing to my niece Liliana. Did you have any luck with the shoe shop, sire?"

"No," the prince said. "But this young lady wants to help us."

"Hi, I'm Kara, the shoemakers' daughter," Kara said.

Barth laughed, but it sounded like a hiccup. "We have all the help we need," he said. "What is the saying? 'Too many cooks ruin the recipe'?"

"Too many cooks spoil the stew," Zed chimed in as he hurried over to Kara.

The prince's dog sniffed Zed's feet. Zed scratched Duncan's ears as the dog licked his shoe.

"Perhaps Barth is right," the prince said. "But thank you for your kind offer, Kara." He patted the carriage seat. "Hop up, Duncan."

Duncan licked Zed's shoe one last time. Then he jumped into the carriage, followed by the prince. The driver shut the carriage door, and they were off.

Kara watched them disappear down the road.

"I'm sorry," Zed said. "I know you were hoping for an adventure."

“The prince *does* need my help,” Kara insisted. “After we get the slipper back, he’ll see I was right.”

“What do you mean *we*?” Zed asked.

Kara smiled. “I’m going to find the stolen slipper, and you’re coming with me.”

4
A New Ball

"Why do we have to find the slipper?" Zed asked.

"Because it'll be fun, and we'll help the prince live happily ever after," Kara said. But she could tell he wasn't sold. "And Prince Patrick will invite us to his wedding. You know what they have at royal weddings?"

Zed's eyes lit up. "Food?"

"Lots of it," Kara said. "So you'll help me?"

Zed sighed. "Yes."

"Come on!" she cried, pulling him away from the shop.

"Wait," Zed said. "We need to tell your parents where we're going."

Kara stopped. Her mother and father would want her to make new shoes, not hunt for old ones.

Before Kara could think of a plan—

Oof! Zed let out a loud groan.

"What's wrong?" Kara asked.

"My bag suddenly got so heavy!" he said.

Zed opened it. Inside, dozens of scrolls had appeared. *It's so unfair*, Kara thought. *Zed travels all over the kingdom* and *he has a magical bag!*

“This one is addressed to my family!” Kara unrolled it. “It says there’s going to be another ball at the castle so that Prince Patrick can choose his bride.”

“What if the mystery lady doesn’t come back for this ball?” Zed asked. His eyes widened. “What if the prince has to marry someone who doesn’t like dogs?”

“We need to find the slipper before the ball so she’ll be there,” Kara said.

"Help!" Kara's mother called from the door. "This goat is eating my curtains!"

Kara and Zed rushed back into the shop. "Mom! There's going to be another ball," Kara said. She handed her mother the scroll.

"This means every girl in the village will want new shoes!" her mother said.

"Do you need me at the shop?" Kara asked. "I was going to help Zed deliver messages."

"No, you two can run along," her mother said. "Your father and I have a lot of ankle bows to sew!"

Nina let out a loud belch.

"But put that goat in the yard first!" Kara's mother added.

"Come on, Nina," Zed said. They led her outside and waved good-bye.

Then Kara and Zed turned toward the castle, ready for their adventure.

5 Mama Zed

Kara and Zed had barely left the shoe shop when Zed stopped walking. “Kara, look!” He pointed to a red squirrel on the side of the road. “The poor thing looks lost.”

“It’s fine, Zed. Come on,” Kara urged. But Zed already had the squirrel on his shoulder. It climbed into Zed’s hair and curled into a ball.

“Aw, she thinks I’m her mommy!” Zed said. “I’ll call her Red. She can come on our adventure!”

"All right, Mama Zed," Kara said, rolling her eyes. "How many deliveries do you have inside the castle?"

Zed flipped through his messenger bag. "There's one for a knight and one for a lady."

"Perfect!" Kara said. "We'll have plenty of time to see inside the prince's library."

"But the slipper is gone. What would we look for in the prince's library?" Zed asked.

"Clues, of course!" Kara said.

They rushed through the village delivering messages. The elf farmer and pixie merchant only thanked them. But the baker's son gave them each a cupcake.

"Yum!" Zed said.

"*Now* I know why you like being a royal messenger," Kara said.

Finally they came to the castle gate. Two ogres stood guard. They saw Zed's royal messenger bag and waved him through.

After Kara and Zed crossed the drawbridge, they came to a busy marketplace. It bustled with people and magical creatures alike. Kara dragged Zed away from the fairy food stalls. Then she dragged herself away from a goblin selling old maps.

Finally they came to the staircase that led to Prince Patrick's castle.

Kara looked up at the castle with her mouth open. *This castle is huge*, she thought. *How will we find any clues here?*

Mr. Murphy

Zed didn't seem to notice the castle. He was looking at a gnome trimming a nearby rosebush. "That's Mr. Murphy, the royal gardener," Zed said. "He took in one of my kittens."

"If he works here," Kara said, "then we should talk to him."

"About the kitten?" Zed asked.

"About the shoe!" Kara dragged him over to the gnome. "Hello, Mr. Murphy. Were you here last week when the glass slipper was stolen?"

The gnome straightened up. "How do you know about that?"

"Prince Patrick told us," Kara said. "We're helping him find it."

Mr. Murphy glanced at Zed and then up at the squirrel on his head. "I know you. You're the boy with all the animals."

"That's right, sir," Zed said. "So *were* you here the day the slipper was stolen?"

Mr. Murphy wiped his forehead. "Yes. I was cleaning up the mess on the stairs."

"Mess?" Kara repeated.

"There were piles of dirt all over," he said. "It took me forever to sweep them. The prince's puppy kept getting underfoot."

"Where did the dirt come from?" Zed asked.

Mr. Murphy pointed to some half-dead roses. "My money's on a gopher. It keeps digging holes in the garden!"

"Oh," Kara said, disappointed. Dirty stairs and gophers weren't much to go on.

"The creature is gone now," the gnome went on. "All those people looking for their fancy stolen gloves scared it away."

"Gloves?" Kara asked. "I thought only the glass slipper was taken."

Mr. Murphy shook his head. "No. Gloves were stolen from the ball, too."

Kara frowned. Who would steal gloves during the ball and come back days later for a glass slipper?

Mr. Murphy turned to Zed. "Do you have any more animals that need homes?"

"I sure do! How do you feel about hedgehogs?" Zed asked.

"They're not the cuddliest, but that's all right," Mr. Murphy replied. "Bring one by the gardening shed tomorrow evening."

"Yes, sir!" Zed said.

"Mr. Murphy," Kara said. "Could you point us toward the prince's library?"

"Yes, it's on the second floor of that tower," Mr. Murphy said. He pointed to a far corner of the castle.

Kara and Zed thanked him and then went to deliver the last two messages. When Zed's messenger bag was finally empty, Zed asked, "Can we go home now? I'm hungry."

"Not yet," Kara said. "We still need to see inside the prince's library." She dragged him around the corner of the castle.

They stared up at the windows of the tower. Thick curtains stared back at them.

Suddenly a dog barked nearby. The sound startled Zed's squirrel. Red jumped out of his hair and scurried up a tree.

"Red!" Zed called. "Come back!"

"She went in through the tower window!" Kara said. From the ground, the window had looked closed. But now Kara saw the curtains blowing in the wind.

"Why are you smiling?" Zed asked.

"Your squirrel just showed us a way into the prince's library!" Kara said. "How are you at climbing trees?"

7

Keep Watch

"No way," Zed said. "I'm not going up there!"

Kara peered at the tower window. "All right," she said. "I'll climb up by myself."

She swung her feet onto one of the low branches and then started to climb. When Kara got to the library window, she stopped.

"I can't get inside!" she called down to Zed. "The window is too far away!"

"Please don't try to jump!" Zed pleaded from the ground below. "Just find Red and come down!"

Kara studied the outside of the window. "This window has a lock, but there's ivy growing around it. I don't think the lock works," Kara said. "I bet someone taller could have reached the window from this branch, climbed inside the library, and stolen the slipper."

"But who? And why?" Zed called back.

"I don't know," Kara said. "I'm going to get a better look. Keep watch!"

"Be careful!" Zed begged. Then he crept along the wall and stood at the corner.

Kara climbed farther onto the branch and squinted through the window. There was a desk overflowing with scrolls and walls full of dusty books. She noticed a glass case in the corner with a crown and scepter inside. Beside the crown sat an empty velvet pillow. *Is that where the slipper was before it was stolen?* Kara wondered.

She heard a chirp inside the room. Red was sitting on the top of a bookcase.

"*Pssssst!* Red!" Kara called. "Come back outside!"

But at that moment, the door to the library burst open.

8
In the Library

Kara ducked down on the branch. She couldn't see into the library, but she could hear two men's voices inside. It was the prince and his chief adviser, Barth.

"Why must we have another ball?" Prince Patrick asked. "Once I find the stolen slipper, I will be able to look for its owner again and—"

"Your Highness," Barth cut in. "Plenty of young ladies would love to be the next princess. My niece, for example, is a fine girl."

"But the one from the ball was clever and funny. I've never met anyone like her!" The prince groaned. "Why didn't she tell me her name before she ran off?"

"My niece Liliana has a lovely name," Barth said.

That's strange, Kara thought. *Why does Barth keep talking about his niece?*

Suddenly Kara heard a chirp. *Oh no. Red!*

“What is this *tree rat* doing in here?” Barth asked.

“The squirrel must have come in through the open window,” Prince Patrick said. “I need to ask Mr. Murphy to trim those vines.”

“I’ll go see him after dinner tomorrow, sire,” Barth said. “It’s not safe to leave your window unlocked when there’s a thief on the loose.”

Kara heard footsteps. Then—*squeak!*—Barth tossed poor Red outside.

The squirrel landed on a branch and dashed away. Kara didn’t dare move. A moment later—*CLICK!* She heard the library door close.

Kara saw a blur of red fur in the branches below. It was Red! Kara climbed down the tree after the squirrel.

A moment later, Kara spotted Duncan, the prince's puppy, bounding toward her. He had Zed's messenger bag in his mouth!

Duncan dropped the bag at Kara's feet. Then he started to dig.

"Kara, quick! Get my bag!" Zed cried, running toward her. "I don't want him to bury it!"

"Sorry, puppy," Kara said as she picked it up.

Duncan whimpered. Then he spotted a cat across the grass and forgot all about the bag. He gave a happy bark and ran off.

"So?" Zed asked, panting. "Did you see any clues in the prince's library?"

"No," she said, smiling. "But I know who took the glass slipper."

Where Is It Hidden?

"I think Barth took the slipper," Kara said.

"Why would *Barth* want it?" Zed asked.

"He wants the prince to marry his niece," Kara said. "He keeps telling Prince Patrick that she'd make a good princess. Without the slipper, the prince won't be able to find the lady from the ball. Barth thinks he'll give up and choose his niece instead."

"But if Barth stole the slipper, did he also steal the gloves from the ball?" Zed asked. "It doesn't make sense."

"No, it doesn't," Kara agreed. "Maybe we're looking for *two* thieves."

"So what do we do?" Zed asked.

"We'll tell the prince about Barth, of course!" Kara said.

Zed shook his head. "He won't believe us. Barth has been the prince's chief adviser for years. We're just a pair of kids."

"You're right. We need proof," Kara said. "We need to find the stolen slipper."

"What if Barth smashed it?" Zed asked. "It *is* made of glass."

Kara hadn't thought of that. "We'll have to follow him to know for sure. He's going to meet with Mr. Murphy tomorrow after dinner," Kara said. "Luckily we'll be at the castle dropping off a hedgehog."

Suddenly Kara's neck prickled as though she were being watched. She glanced around, but no one was there.

Something chirped nearby. A moment later, Red jumped back into Zed's hair.

"Red!" Zed said. "There you are."

Kara glanced at the setting sun. Her parents would expect her home soon. The search for the slipper would have to wait.

She and Zed headed back to the drawbridge. As they passed an empty cart, Kara noticed someone hiding behind it. It was a teenage girl in fancy clothes and shining braids.

The girl was staring right at them.

"Zed," Kara whispered. "I think we're being watched."

Partners in Crime Solving

"We're being watched?" Zed said. "By who?"

The stranger must have heard him. She turned and rushed down a narrow alley.

"Oh, her," Zed said to Kara. "I saw her sneaking around when you were in that tree."

"I wonder who she is," Kara said.

The alley where the girl had disappeared was empty. Zed's stomach rumbled. The sad sound echoed off the alley walls.

"I told you I was hungry," Zed said with a shrug.

"All right, let's go home," Kara said.

A short walk later, they were back at the shoe shop.

"See you tomorrow for the hedgehog drop-off!" Kara said.

They grinned at each other. Then Zed headed off to his cottage.

Inside the shop, Kara's parents were still working on new shoe designs.

"Kara!" her father said. "You were gone so long, we thought you'd run off to the Dragon Lands."

"Not this time. I went along with Zed to deliver invitations to the ball," Kara said.

"I hope the prince finds his mystery girl," her mother said. "Then I can find out who made her glass slippers!"

"Do you think a shoe like that could break?" Kara asked.

Her father chuckled. "I doubt it. Fairy magic can survive anything!"

So Barth couldn't *have smashed the slipper,* Kara thought. *He must have hidden it. And tomorrow, I have to find out where.*

11 Follow Barth!

Kara spent the next day cutting and molding and stitching. *Finding missing shoes is a lot more fun than making them*, she decided.

That evening, Zed came to the shop. He was holding his stomach.

"Did you eat too much of your gram's pie again?" Kara asked. She jumped when his shirt moved on its own!

"The baby hedgehog climbed down my shirt," Zed said. "Ouch! He keeps poking me!"

Kara waved good-bye to her parents. They looked so happy surrounded by shoes and customers. Kara was happy, too. This was the life for her: mysteries, excitement, and adventure!

At the drawbridge, Kara and Zed told the two guards they were back to see Mr. Murphy.

The taller ogre laughed. "Did the royal gardener find his glove-stealing gopher?"

"I bet its paws were cold," the shorter guard joked.

The ogres kept laughing as Kara and Zed crossed the drawbridge.

It was late in the day, so the marketplace was closing up. As Kara gazed longingly toward the maps again, she noticed something.

"Zed, look!" she whispered. "It's Barth!"

The prince's adviser hurried through the marketplace as if he were late for something.

Kara turned to Zed. "Go meet Mr. Murphy. I'll follow Barth."

"No way," Zed said. "I'm coming with you."

There was no time to argue. Kara and Zed followed Barth to a small garden.

They ducked behind some bushes. Kara hoped Barth would lead them to the glass slipper. Instead, he sat on a bench.

"What is he doing?" Zed whispered.

Kara was wondering the same thing. "It looks like he's waiting for something."

"Or someone," Zed added.

Part of the Plan

A few minutes later, a hooded figure hurried into the garden.

"Well, Liliana?" Barth demanded. "You took long enough!"

The figure pushed back the hood. Kara saw it was the girl who had been watching them yesterday!

"Liliana is Barth's niece!" she whispered to Zed.

"Did you find it?" Barth asked his niece.

"No, Uncle," Liliana said. "I looked all around the castle tower, but it wasn't there. Why did you throw it out the library window instead of hiding it in a safe place?"

"The prince barged into his library, and I had to think fast." Barth huffed. "Now it's gone."

"Why does it even matter?" Liliana asked. "Without the slipper, the prince can't find the lady from the ball."

"That may be true. But we don't know where the slipper is now. What if it gets back to the mystery lady somehow? That will ruin our plan," Barth said.

"*Your* plan, Uncle," Liliana said. "I didn't ask to be part of it."

"But you *are* part of it," Barth said. "You will be the next princess, and I will help you rule the kingdom."

Kara could hardly breathe. “We have to go tell the prince about this,” she whispered to Zed.

At that moment, the hedgehog in Zed’s shirt must have stretched his quills. “Ow!” Zed shrieked.

Barth and Liliana froze. Then Barth charged toward the bushes.

“Run!” Kara cried. But it was too late.

13
Caught!

"What are you doing?" Barth demanded. He held Kara's and Zed's arms so they couldn't run.

"Um. We're on our way to meet Mr. Murphy," Zed said.

"But . . . we got lost," Kara said.

Barth turned to Liliana, who looked on nervously. "Stay here until I get back," he told her. Then he dragged Kara and Zed away.

Even though Barth was a small man, he must have been part ogre. Kara struggled to get free, but it was no use.

"Where are you taking us?" Kara asked.

"To see Mr. Murphy?" Zed asked hopefully.

"To see the guards," Barth said. "If I catch you on the castle grounds again, I'll throw you and your families in the dungeons."

Kara imagined her poor parents locked up. She couldn't tell Prince Patrick about Barth's plan now!

Barth delivered Kara and Zed to the guards at the drawbridge. "Make sure these two never set foot in the castle again," he told them.

This time, the guards weren't laughing. The ogres dragged them across the moat and dumped them on the road.

“But I’m a royal messenger!” Zed cried. The guards didn’t seem to hear him. “Can you at least make sure Mr. Murphy gets this hedgehog?” He cradled the creature in his hands.

The guards only snorted and marched away.

“I can’t believe it,” Kara said. “We tried to help the prince, and we failed.”

“At least now we know that Barth stole the slipper,” Zed pointed out.

Kara gave the ground an angry kick. “Yes, but we still don’t know where it is. Without that glass slipper, Barth is going to get away with his plan.”

“We can’t give up,” Zed said.

Kara’s shoulders slumped. “I’m not sure what else we can do,” she said. “Let’s go home.”

14 What Else Can We Do?

As Kara and Zed left the castle gates, someone called out from behind them: "Wait!"

It was Liliana. "I need your help!" she said. "I have to stop Uncle Barth."

"Why should we believe you?" Zed asked.

"I believe her," Kara said. "Liliana could have told Barth earlier that she saw us yesterday. But she didn't."

"If Barth finds out you're looking for the slipper, he'll put you in the dungeon," Liliana said. "That's where he's keeping my mother and father—his own sister and her husband!—until I marry the prince."

"He wants you to become the next princess so that he can control the prince?" Zed asked.

"Yes, but I don't want to be a princess. I don't like being in the spotlight or dressing up," Liliana said. "Besides, I can't get in the way of Prince Patrick marrying his true love."

"But how can we help?" Zed asked. "We're banished from the castle."

"*Someone* has to stop my uncle before the ball tomorrow," Liliana said.

Kara thought for a minute. "I have a plan!" she said. "Liliana, get ready for some shoe shopping. And Zed, we need to deliver a message to the prince."

"But we're not allowed inside the castle," Zed said. "How can we bring him a message?"

Kara smiled. "*We* can't, but your hedgehog can!"

15

Try on All the Shoes

In the morning, Kara couldn't sit still. She was worried that Prince Patrick hadn't gotten their message. If her plan to catch Barth failed, the prince might end up with the wrong girl at the ball tonight!

"Sweeping the floor again?" her mother asked. "Are you feeling all right?"

"Fine!" Kara said. "I want the shop to look nice in case we get important visitors."

Oops. Kara had said too much. She glanced at the clock. "Mom! I think I hear Dad calling you from the storeroom."

"He might need help gluing heels," her mother said. She headed toward the back of the shop.

Just then, the front door jingled as it opened. Prince Patrick strode inside.

"Sire!" Kara said, sinking into a curtsy. "I was afraid you wouldn't get our message in time."

"Murphy said the note was attached to a hedgehog's paw?" Prince Patrick asked.

"It was the only way to get it to you," Kara said. Last night, Liliana had left the hedgehog on the royal gardener's doorstep with a secret letter for the prince. It had asked him to come to the shoe shop the next day, alone and on foot.

"The message said that you know where the stolen glass slipper is," said the prince.

"Not exactly," Kara replied. "But I do know who took it."

"Who?" the prince asked.

Kara heard a carriage outside the shop. "It's best if you see the truth for yourself, sire," Kara said. "That's why we need to hide."

"Hide?" Prince Patrick repeated.

Kara nodded. "If you want to find your true love, this might be the only way," Kara said.

The prince hesitated. "Very well," he said. Then he ducked behind the counter.

"Mom!" Kara called. "We have a customer!" She crawled behind the counter out of sight as Barth and Liliana came in.

“This place makes the best shoes in the village,” Liliana said. Then she whispered, “And a princess-to-be needs the best shoes. Right, Uncle?”

Kara’s mother came in from the storeroom. “How can I help you?” she asked.

“I need some new shoes for the ball tonight,” Liliana said.

"Expensive shoes," Barth said. "My niece must look like a queen."

"Very well, sir," Kara's mother said, sounding pleased. "What style are you looking for?"

"I'm not sure," Liliana said. "I suppose I should try on *all* your shoes."

"Of course! We have some new ones with bows," Kara's mother said. She rushed back to the storeroom, humming happily to herself.

"I see you've warmed up to my plan," Barth said to his niece.

"You've worked hard for the royal family, Uncle. They should respect you."

"The prince listens to my advice, but he doesn't always do what I tell him," Barth hissed. "When I have you whispering ideas in Prince Patrick's ear, I will finally have complete control of the kingdom!"

The prince gasped softly. He looked ready to storm out of hiding, but Kara put her hand on his arm.

"I only hope my parents can attend the wedding," Liliana went on.

"We'll see," Barth said.

"Please, Uncle," Liliana said. "I've done everything you've asked. Can't you let my parents out of the dungeons?"

At that, the prince jumped to his feet. "I have heard enough!" he cried.

16
Stop the Thief!

"S-sire!" Barth stammered. "What are—How did—"

"Is this all true?" Prince Patrick demanded. "Did *you* steal the slipper from my library? Did you lock up Liliana's parents?"

Barth only stood with his mouth open.

Kara's mother hurried out of the storeroom. "Who's ready for ankle bows?" she chirped. When she saw the prince, she dropped her armload of shoes. "Your Highness!"

Just then, Barth turned and darted out of the door.

"Stop!" Prince Patrick called. And he took off after him.

Everyone hurried out of the shop as Barth jumped into his carriage. "Drive!" he yelled to the coachman. "Go!"

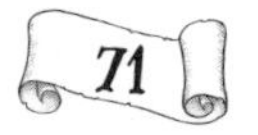

But the carriage didn't move. The coachman took off his hat. Underneath was Zed's smiling face. "Sorry," Zed said. "This horse is taking a break."

"It's over, Barth!" the prince yelled.

But Barth leaped out of the carriage and took off on foot.

"He's getting away!" Kara called.

Then she heard barking. A blur of brown zipped by her. Kara watched, amazed, as Duncan pinned Barth to the ground.

"Get off me!" Barth yelled as Duncan chewed on his necktie.

"Barth," Prince Patrick said. "You must leave my kingdom at once! But first, tell me where the glass slipper is."

"I don't know," Barth said. "I threw it out your library window. When I went to find it, it was gone!"

"Do you expect me to believe such a story?" the prince asked.

"He's telling the truth, sire," Kara said.

The prince's face fell. "Then the slipper may really be gone forever."

Duncan finally yanked off Barth's tie. He bounded away, dug a hole in the ground, and dropped the necktie inside.

Kara sucked in a breath. "Sire! I know where the slipper is!"

Dig In

"You think *Duncan* took the slipper and hid it?" Prince Patrick asked.

"Yes, sire," Kara said. "After Barth threw it out the window, Duncan must have picked it up. If we go to the castle, I'll show you where it is."

Prince Patrick looked doubtful, but he said, "You were right about Barth. Perhaps you're right about this, too."

"I guess this means we're not banished from the castle anymore," Zed whispered to Kara as they climbed into the royal carriage.

At the castle, Kara asked for the royal gardener. But when they explained Kara's hunch to Mr. Murphy, he was not happy.

"You want to dig up my roses?" he asked. "Hasn't that gopher done enough?"

"There's no gopher," Kara said. "Duncan has been digging these holes."

"Listen to Kara, please," the prince said. Then he took Liliana aside and called over one of his guards. "Help this girl find her parents. Make sure they're set free."

"Right away, Your Highness," the ogre said.

"Thank you, Kara and Zed," Liliana said. "I hope you find the slipper—and the prince's true love."

Then she hurried off to the dungeons.

Kara took a deep breath. She hoped she was right about the slipper.

Kara, Zed, and Prince Patrick began shoveling dirt. Duncan wagged his tail as he helped. Mr. Murphy covered his eyes, unable to watch.

They dug and dug and dug. Kara started to wonder if she'd made a mistake. Then her shovel hit something.

"It's a scarf!" She pulled it out of the dirt. Underneath was a chewed-up bone.

"I found gloves over here!" Zed called.

Those had to be the ones taken from the ball! Duncan had stowed them in his favorite hiding spot.

Kara kept digging. Finally—*ding!*—her shovel hit something hard.

She pulled the object out of the dirt. It was covered in soil, but it still sparkled.

"I found it," she whispered.

Prince Patrick gently took the slipper from her. He wiped it on his shirt, leaving a streak across his heart. Kara had never seen such a perfect shoe.

"Now I can go find my true love," the prince said. "Thank you, Kara and Zed." He hurried toward his horse.

Kara's head was spinning. They'd found the stolen slipper!

18

A Perfect Fit

The prince found his princess that same day. Her name was Cinderella. The glass slipper fit her perfectly, and she had another one just like it. Prince Patrick turned the ball that night into an engagement party. And he invited the whole kingdom—even Nina!

Kara walked into the ballroom with her parents. All three of them wore new shoes, with ankle bows, of course.

She waved to Zed at the buffet table. He had filled up one plate for himself and one for Nina. The goat looked fancy in her bow.

“Kara!” Zed said. “Don’t tell my gram, but these cheese tarts are even better than hers.”

"Where *is* your gram?" Kara asked.

He pointed to the dance floor. "She's dancing with Mr. Murphy." Gram and the royal gardener spun and twirled. The hedgehog peeked out of Mr. Murphy's pocket.

Just then, Prince Patrick came by with Cinderella at his side. "Kara and Zed, without your help, I never would have found my princess," he said.

"And I never would have found my prince," Cinderella said. She smiled as Duncan ran by with a sock in his mouth. "Or my new favorite dog."

"Come back with that!" Prince Patrick cried, dashing after him. Cinderella laughed and hurried off, too.

"See, Zed? You didn't have to worry," Kara said. "Cinderella loves dogs."

Around them, the ballroom echoed with music and happiness. Kara breathed it all in. "We did it," she said. "We solved the big mystery."

“Now what?” Zed asked.

“We try some of that cherry pie,” Kara said.

Zed looked surprised.

“Isn’t there a castle to break into or a bad guy to find?” Zed asked.

“Let’s have dessert first.” Kara smiled. “We can have another adventure tomorrow.”

ABOUT THE CREATORS

Anna Staniszewski is the author of over a dozen books for young readers, including *Secondhand Wishes* and *Dogosauraus Rex*. She lives outside of Boston with her family and teaches at Simmons University. She shares both Kara's love of reading and Zed's love of ice cream.

Macky Pamintuan was born in the Philippines. He received his bachelor of fine arts in San Francisco, and he has illustrated numerous children's books. He has a smarty pants young daughter who loves to read and go on imaginary adventures with her furry pal and trusty sidekick, Winter. He now lives in Mexico with his family.

Questions and Activities

A lot happens to Cinderella's missing shoe in this story! What happens to the shoe first? What happens second? Reread chapters 12 and 17 to find the answers.

Duncan likes to steal clothes and bury them. Name at least three things he buries in the story.

Why does Liliana want to stop her Uncle Barth's plan? Find at least two reasons given in the story.

In chapter 15, Kara and Zed leave a note for Prince Patrick. What special way do they deliver the note?

Prince Patrick searches for his true love's lost shoe. Pretend one of your favorite shoes has gone missing. Draw a picture of the shoe—just like Prince Patrick did—so people can help you find it!